FOR ELIZABETH AND TERRY — SR
FOR LIZ T — ET

First published in Great Britain in 2000 by Bloomsbury Publishing Plc
38 Soho Square, London W1V 5DF

Text copyright © Shen Roddie 2000
Illustrations copyright © Eleanor Taylor 2000
The moral right of the author and illustrator has been asserted.

A CIP catalogue record for this book is available from the British Library.
ISBN 0 7475 4775 0

Printed in Singapore by Tien Wah Press Pte Ltd

1 3 5 7 9 10 8 6 4 2

Whoever's Heard of a Hibernating Pig

Shen Roddie and Eleanor Taylor

BLOOMSBURY
CHILDREN'S
BOOKS

'Whee!' squealed Pig as he plopped onto his sledge and whooshed down the slope to Hedgehog's house.

'Hedgehog!' called Pig. 'Come out and play!'
But there was no reply. A sign beside a pile of cones said, 'Nighty-Night! Call back in spring.'
'Bother!' said Pig.

'Tortoise!' shouted Pig. 'Come out and play!'
But there was no reply. A note on an old pot said,
'Sleeping through winter. Wake me in spring.'
'Lazybones,' grumbled Pig.

'Squirrel!' yelled Pig.
'Come out and play!'

Shushh!
owner
hibernating

But there was no reply. A sign by the tree trunk said,
'Shushh! Owner hibernating.'

'Dormouse!' hollered Pig.
'Are you asleep, too? If not come out and play!'

'Fee-Feew! Sss..oorr!' came the reply.
Pig looked in. Dormouse was in bed and snoring.

'But spring is months away!' groaned Pig.
'Why!' said Pig suddenly perking up. 'I'll join them! I'll sleep
through winter. Then we can all wake up in spring and
play! Oinkidoo,' whooped Pig, leaping heavily into the air.
He stuck a sign outside his door. It said simply:
Hibernating Pig.

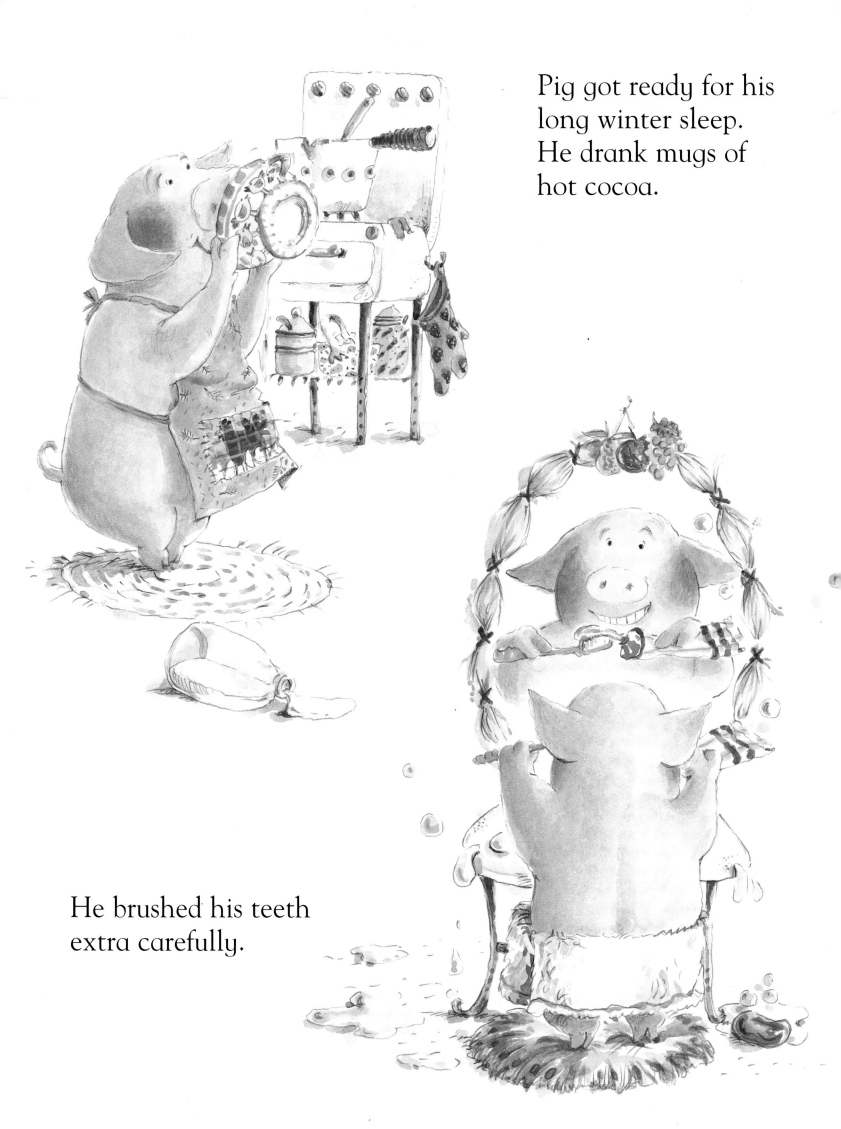

Pig got ready for his
long winter sleep.
He drank mugs of
hot cocoa.

He brushed his teeth
extra carefully.

He put on two pairs of extra-warm pyjamas.

He jumped into bed and tucked himself under three warm blankets.

Pig lay still
for a long time.
Slowly he opened
one eye,
then another.
'It's hard to sleep when
you're not sleepy,' he said.
'Yawning should make
me sleepy,' yawned Pig.
But it didn't.

Pig fluffed his pillow.
    'It's hard to sleep when you're not comfortable,' said Pig.
    He made himself very comfortable (with plenty of pillows).
Still he could not sleep.

Pig lay very still for a very long time. He listened.

He heard the clock tick.

He heard the tap drip.

He heard low
rumbling noises.

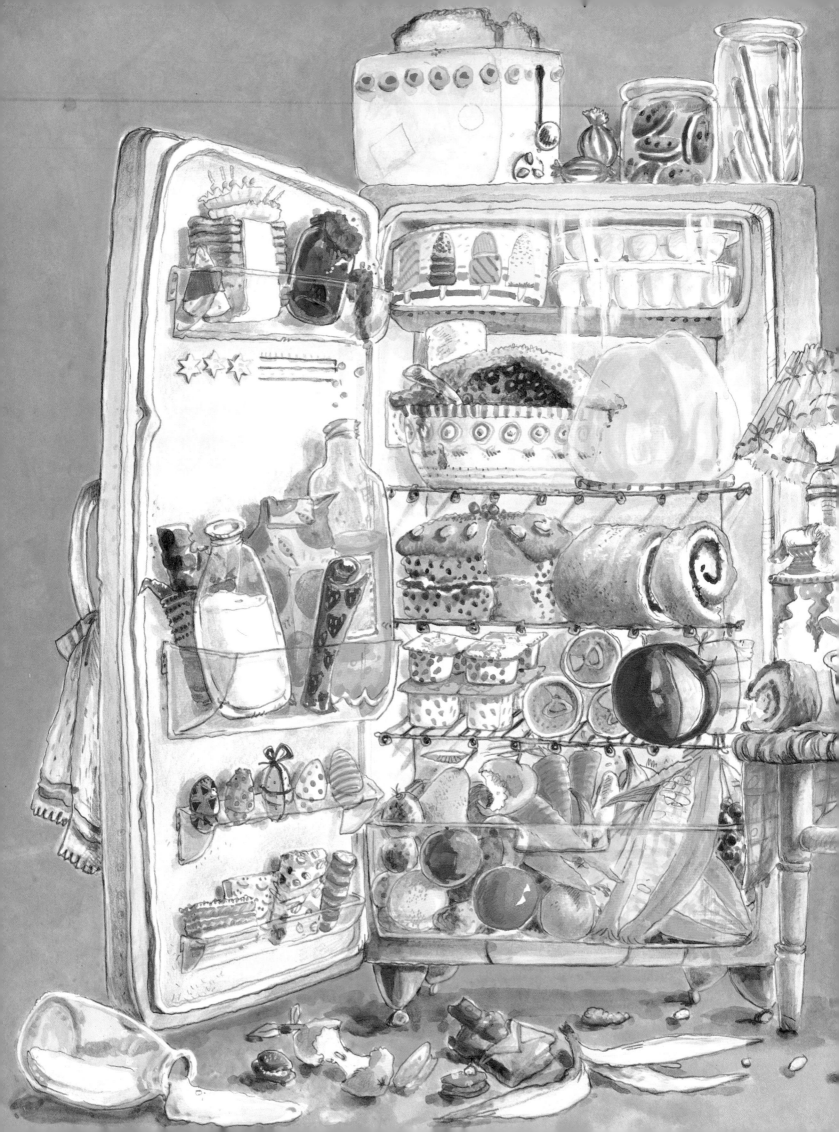

'That's my tummy! It's hard to sleep when you're hungry,'
said Pig, getting out of bed. 'I need a snack.'
Pig fixed himself a stack of really yummy sandwiches.
'Delicious!' said Pig, his stomach nice and warm and full.

'Now I can go back to sleep. Goodnight, winter!' said Pig, climbing back into bed.

He hummed and whistled and twiddled his thumbs.

'I'm bored, bored, bored!' said Pig, picking at his blanket. He pulled out a bit of wool. Then a little bit more. The wool grew longer and longer as his blanket grew shorter and shorter.

'I think I like hibernating!' Pig said.

Soon there was nothing left but a pile of fluffy blue wool.
That night, Pig slept like a beanbag.

But the next day Pig was as wide awake as ever!
Pig counted spiders and cobwebs. Still he could not sleep.

'My blanket!' cried Pig, remembering what fun he'd had with it. Pig sat up in bed. He picked at his other blankets, pulling out a bit of wool. Then a little bit more. He plucked at them all day. Soon there was nothing left but two woolly lumps.

Pig looked up. The ground was still thick with snow.

'Blow it,' huffed Pig. 'What does a pig do when he has trouble hibernating?'

'Why!' Pig cried suddenly. 'He gets ready for spring, of course!'

With that, Pig went to get his knitting needles and began to knit.
Click! Click! Click!

Pig lay in bed and knitted for weeks and weeks!
'Just like sleeping through winter!' laughed Pig.

By the time Pig had finished knitting it was spring.
The daffodils were out and dancing.

'Pig!' cried Hedgehog, Tortoise, Squirrel and Dormouse in their loudest, jolliest and most wide-awake voices. 'Wake up! It's spring! Come out and play!'

'Coming!' cried Pig, jumping out of bed.

'What shall we play, Pig?' they asked.

A big woolly thing shot out of the front door.
'How about catch!'
shouted Pig, and they laughed as they
raced down the hill
after it.